NEVER PAPA BEAR
A Book About SIGNS

By Mabel Watts
Illustrated by Art Seiden

🌹 A GOLDEN BOOK · NEW YORK

rhcbooks.com
Educators and librarians, for a variety of teaching tools, visit us at RHTeachersLibrarians.com
Library of Congress Control Number: 2020945373
ISBN 978-0-593-30657-4 (trade) — ISBN 978-0-593-30658-1 (ebook)
Printed in the United States of America
10 9 8 7 6 5 4 3 2 1

Signs! Signs!

Everywhere I look, I see signs looking back at me. They tell me when things are going to happen, what to look for, where to go, and how to get there.

Do you see a sign that is just right for you?

A sign can be a warning. It tells me to keep my eyes wide open and *look*!

When I don't read warning signs, I sometimes get into trouble!

Some of the nicest signs are invitations. I *like* those signs.

A sign can be a question, too.

If you guess the right number of jelly beans,
you'll win a prize!

Sometimes signs answer questions.
There are many answer signs at the zoo.

STRAIGHT
AHEAD FOR
LION
HOUSE

Other signs make me hungry.
Do they make you hungry, too?

CROSS HERE

Keep Off the Grass

A sign can be an order. It tells me what to do and what not to do.

It's best to obey order signs, but sometimes it isn't easy.

Some signs give advice. Here is some good advice.

A sign can be a rhyme, too. Rhyming signs are fun to say over and over.

Which rhyme do you like best?

Oh, yes, and a sign can be a joke. I watch for signs that make me laugh.

It takes lots of signs to help people get from one place to another.

Can you follow these signs to find your way across town?

There! You did it! Now turn the page, and
you'll see that the signs have led you right to . . .